This Storybook Belongs to:

Princess __Taylor Rose__

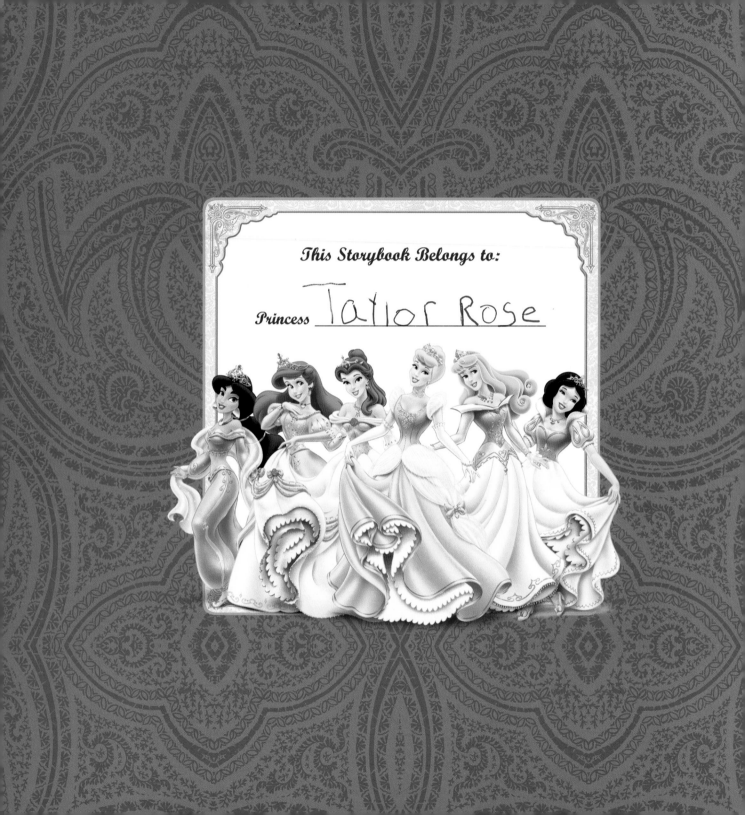

Snow White
and the Seven Dwarfs

A Gift from the Heart

Enchanted Moments

Advance
PUBLISHERS

Snow White was as happy as could be. She was married to her true love, the Prince, and lived in a beautiful castle where everyone treated her with respect and kindness. Even so, she couldn't help missing her dear friends the Seven Dwarfs.

"It's high time you paid them a visit," declared the Prince. "Why don't we ride over this afternoon?"

"What a splendid idea!" Snow White replied.

When she and the Prince arrived at the cottage in the woods, however, the Dwarfs were not at home. Snow White decided to bake them some gooseberry pies while she waited.

"Have a wonderful time," the Prince told her as he rode off on official royal business. "I'll return for our journey home at sunset."

As the Dwarfs returned home that afternoon, the mouth-watering smell of pie wafted out of the cottage to greet them.

"Snow White must be here!" they exclaimed. They soon spotted the Princess visiting with some forest creatures nearby.

After the old friends had exchanged greetings, the Dwarfs wanted to know all about what life was like at the castle.

"Are there lots of bancy falls—I mean *fancy balls*?" wondered Doc.

"Oh, yes!" Snow White replied. "Would you like to attend one sometime?"

Her friends nodded their heads enthusiastically. "How about now?" asked Happy.

Snow White laughed. "Well, there isn't a ball being held at the castle today . . . but I know someplace else where we might find one."

"Follow me," said Snow White as she led the Dwarfs back to the cottage. "I think there's a ball about to begin right now!"

"Hmmph!" said Grumpy. "Then where is the orchestra? And where are the guests?"

"Silly Grumpy!" Snow White exclaimed. "They're right inside this room!"

Now the Dwarfs understood! They got out their instruments and began to play. The ball had begun! The friends danced together to tune after lively tune until the sun began to lower in the sky.

"That was delightful, Princess," said Doc. "It reminds me of all the tood gimes, I mean good rhymes, I mean *good times* we had when you first came to live with us as the cottage."

"I have many fond memories of all of you, too," Snow White replied, "but right now it's time for me to get back to the castle." She gave each Dwarf a kiss on the head goodbye. When it was Dopey's turn, he held up his hands in the shape of a heart. "And I love you, Dopey," Snow White told him. Then she formed a heart with her hands, too.

Soon the Prince arrived to escort Snow White back home. Before the couple left, however, the Prince quietly asked Grumpy if he could speak with him for a moment.

"Snow White misses you all so much," the Prince told him, "so tomorrow, as a special surprise, I'd like you all to join us for a picnic in the woods."

"You can count on us to be there," Grumpy told the Prince. "And we'll even wash up first!"

Now the Prince realized just how much Grumpy cared for Snow White. Grumpy hated washing up more than anything!

The next morning at work, Doc and Grumpy decided the Dwarfs should give Snow White a special gift at the picnic.

"That way, when she's back at the tassle, I mean the *castle*, she'll have something to remind her of all of us," said Doc.

"But what should we give her?" asked Grumpy.

"It has to be beautiful, like the Princess," said Doc. "And it should last forever, just like our love for her."

They both looked at each other and smiled. "A diamond!" they exclaimed, and headed back into the mine to find just the right one.

Doc and Grumpy didn't know it, but Dopey had been listening to their conversation. He agreed that a diamond would make a nice gift for Snow White—but it couldn't be just any diamond. It had to be as special as Snow White herself.

All of Dopey's memories of Snow White came rushing back to him—
and suddenly he knew exactly where to find a gift worthy of his friend.

Dopey ventured back into the mine and went straight to a diamond he had spotted earlier that morning. The gem was huge, and its facets sparkled even in the darkness. But what made the diamond unique beyond compare was that it was shaped exactly like a heart!

"Dopey!" cried the other Dwarfs as they stumbled upon their friend. "You did it! You found the perfect gift for the Princess!"

Dopey smiled, then turned, lifted his axe into the air—and broke the heart-shaped diamond in two!

"Oh, no!" Doc groaned.

"Dopey!" cried Grumpy. "Why did you go and do that for? Snow White and the Prince will be here any minute. Now what are we going to give her?"

The Dwarfs raced back to the cottage just in time to greet the royal couple.
"Surprise, Princess!" cried the Dwarfs breathlessly.

The Prince turned to his bride. "We're all going to have a picnic together," he explained.

A radiant smile lit up Snow White's face. "Oh, how wonderful!" she replied.

"Run along," said Doc. "We'll be there in a minute!"

As Snow White walked ahead, Grumpy came flying at the Prince and blocked his way.

"We can't have the picnic yet," he announced. "The gift we had for Snow White . . . Dopey broke it!"

"The only gift Snow White needs is your friendship," the Prince reassured him. "Now come along and let's enjoy our picnic."

As the festivities began, the Prince could see that Grumpy and Doc were each holding a small bag. It seemed they wanted to give them to Snow White.

"What is it?" the Prince asked. "Don't be shy."

"They're for you, Princess," said Doc hesitantly.

"How sweet!" Snow White replied, clapping her hands together in delight. "More surprises!"

"Oh, you'll be surprised, all right," mumbled Grumpy.

Snow White opened the bag and half of Dopey's diamond tumbled out. "Oh, my!" Snow White cried, "it's beautiful."

But Grumpy was embarrassed. A Princess deserved a large, perfect diamond—not a *piece* of one!

Doc looked on fretfully as Snow White opened the second bag. "Another diamond!" she exclaimed. "Why, thank you! I will treasure them always!" Then Snow White noticed that all the Dwarfs—except for Dopey—looked disappointed.

"Whatever is the matter?" she asked.

"Your present," began Doc, "it woke, it spoke, I mean it *broke*. We're sorry."

"I don't understand," Snow White replied.

Dopey stepped forward, took the two pieces of the diamond, and put them together.

"Look!" said Snow White. "A perfect heart!"

"I see," said the Prince to the Dwarfs. "Half the heart represents Snow White and the other half represents all of you."

"And together they show how much we love each other," added Snow White. "Is that right?"

Dopey nodded his head and proudly puffed out his chest.

Now the rest of the Dwarfs understood why Dopey had broken the diamond!

"Sorry we got mad," Grumpy apologized to Dopey.

"Thank you, Dopey," added Doc. "We wanted to give Snow White something truly special— and because of you, we did!"

Late that afternoon, as the royal couple prepared to
return to the castle, Snow White took the Prince's
hands in hers.

"Thank you for planning such a lovely day," she
told him, "I had a wonderful time, and I know my
friends did, too."

"I have a feeling your friendship with them
will last forever," said the Prince. "Just
like the diamond heart!"